USBORNE F...
Leve...

USBORNE FIRST READING

## The Dinosaur Who Lost His ROAR

Russell Punter
Illustrated by Andy Elkerton

USBORNE FIRST READING

## The Castle That Jack Built

Lesley Sims
Illustrated by
Mike Gordon

USBORNE FIRST READING

## Chicken Licken

retold by
Russell Punter
Illustrated by Ann Kronheimer

USBORNE FIRST READING

## The Three Little Pigs

...dson
...Overwater

# Dick Whittington

### Retold by
### Russell Punter

### Illustrated by
### Barbara Vagnozzi

Reading Consultant: Alison Kelly
Roehampton University

There was once a boy called Dick Whittington. He lived on his own, in the country.

Dick was very, very poor.

He had no
money for
fancy clothes...

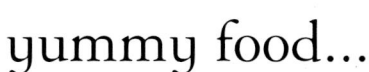 yummy food...

or a warm,
dry home.

"I need a job," he thought.

So he looked for work. He asked boatmen...

builders...

and blacksmiths.

But no one needed help.

One morning, Dick saw a farmer. "Can you give me a job?" he asked.

Sorry, nothing here lad.

"Why not try in London?" said the man.

Dick knew London was a big city, many miles away.

"They say the streets are made of gold," said the farmer.

"Gold!" thought Dick. "I'll be rich." He thanked the farmer and set off at once.

# Dick walked for miles...

and miles...

and miles.

LONDON
50 miles

LONDON
25 miles

LONDON
10 miles

But when he arrived
in London...

...the streets weren't made of
gold at all. "They're just dirty
and smelly," thought Dick.

He looked for work once
more. He asked bakers...

butchers...

and boot
menders.

But no one wanted help.

10

Soon it was dark. Dick needed somewhere to spend the night.

This will have to do.

He curled up on the steps of a big house and fell asleep.

The next morning, Dick woke to hear someone shouting in his ear.

Get off these steps!

A woman stood over him. "Go away!" she yelled.

12

Before Dick could move, a man came out of the house.

"Are you alright, son?" he asked. "Come inside."

Dick had never been in such a grand house before. It was full of beautiful things.

"Welcome to my home," said the man. "My name is Mr. Fitzwarren."

"My ships take things to be sold all over the world."

Mr. Fitzwarren gave Dick a job in his kitchen. Dick spent the day washing pots...

cleaning floors...

and peeling carrots.

It was hard work.

But Dick was happy with his new job. And everyone in the house was kind to him.

# Well, almost everyone...

After his first day's work, Dick was taken to the very top of the house.

You can sleep in the attic, Dick.

The room was small, but
Dick didn't mind.

Just as he began to fall
asleep, he heard a loud
**squeak!**

A mouse squeezed out of a
hole in the floorboards...

Squeak!

followed by
another...

Squeak!

and another.

Squeak!

Seconds later, the whole room was full of mice.

_Squeak!_

_Squeak!_

_Squeak!_

Dick couldn't get a wink of sleep.

It was the same every night.
Just as Dick's head hit the
pillow...

...the mice came out.

The mice drove Dick crazy.
"I must get rid of them,"
he thought.

A week later, Mr. Fitzwarren gave Dick his first ever wages.

Dick couldn't wait to go out and spend his money.

That afternoon, he visited the big city market. There were hundreds of stalls.

Ye cream cakes
5 pennies each

Ye bread rolls
4 for a penny

Ye rhubarb sticks
1 penny a bag

Dick had never seen so many things for sale.

Then he suddenly saw
just what he needed.

🙰 YE PETS 🙰

Puppies
2 pennies
each

Grow your own
frogs
1 penny per jar

Cats
1 penny each

"A cat will keep those noisy
mice away," thought Dick.

He bought the biggest cat
from the stall and ran home.

I'll call
you Tom.

That night, the mice
appeared as usual.

But, this time, Dick was ready for them.

Tom the cat chased the mice back into their holes.

"At last, I can get a good night's sleep," thought Dick.

Dick and his cat curled up and fell fast asleep.

31

A few days later, Mr. Fitzwarren called his servants together.

"One of my ships is going on a selling trip," he said.

"If you have anything you want to sell, it can go on the ship. It sails tonight."

Dick thought for a moment.

He only had one thing to
sell – his cat.

"Maybe someone will give
me two pennies for Tom,"
he thought.

34

Dick put his cat onto the cart that was going to Mr. Fitzwarren's ship.

That evening, Dick couldn't sleep.

He felt bad about selling
Tom. The mice were back too.

Squeak!

Squeak!

The next day, he wandered
around, half asleep.

"Wake up, you lazy boy!" growled the cook. "Work harder."

From then on, she made Dick work twice as hard as anyone else.

She was mean for a month.
"I'm going back to the
country," thought Dick.

Early one morning, he
slipped out of the house.

He walked and walked, until he had almost left London.

Just then, church bells rang out.

"That's strange," thought Dick. "The bells sound like they're calling to me."

Turn again Whittington, thrice mayor of London.

"They're telling me to go back," he realized.

"And they're saying I'll be the mayor — three times. How odd."

Dick could hardly believe
his ears. But he went back to
Mr. Fitzwarren's house.

A surprise was
waiting for him.

"Congratulations, Dick," boomed Mr. Fitzwarren. "You're rich!"

Rich? Me?

"The king of Barbary bought your cat."

"His palace was full of mice
and Tom chased them off."

Mr. Fitzwarren handed Dick
two bags bursting with gold.
"Here you are."

Dick used the money to
buy and sell things, just like
Mr. Fitzwarren.

He grew up to be one of the
richest men in the city.

What's more, the bells were right. Dick did become mayor of London... three times!

*Dick Whittington* is based on the life of a real person who lived from about 1350 to 1423. Richard Whittington was brought up in Gloucestershire, England and went to London to find work. He became a successful cloth merchant and was mayor of London three times.

Series editor: Lesley Sims

First published in 2008 by Usborne Publishing Ltd., Usborne House, 83-85 Saffron Hill, London EC1N 8RT, England. www.usborne.com
Copyright © 2008 Usborne Publishing Ltd.

48

# USBORNE FIRST READING
## Level Four

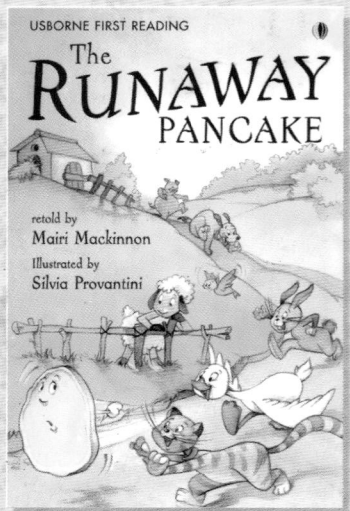